Old Tom's
HOLIDAY

Leigh HOBBS

LITTLE HARE

Angela Throgmorton loved Old Tom, but bringing him up was hard work. He liked to relax, and never helped around the house.

One morning, during breakfast, Angela received some exciting news.
She had won a luxury holiday! Angela was thrilled.
And so was Old Tom. He was *always* in the mood for a holiday.

Angela finished the dishes then packed her bags…

…and Old Tom packed his.

Then, just when he was ready to leave, Old Tom heard some dreadful news.
"It's a trip for one," said Angela Throgmorton. "Why don't you clean
your room while I'm gone?"

Soon Angela was on her way.

She was upset to be leaving Old Tom, of course.

"But there's food in the freezer and I won't be gone for long," Angela told herself.
She settled back and studied her itinerary.

On her first night away, Angela stayed in a grand hotel.
"I'm sure I folded these more carefully," she said, while
unpacking a few of her favourite things.

In the morning, Angela stepped out into a street full of skyscrapers.
She wanted to blend in, so she had her hair done especially.

Angela seemed to be on the move all the time.

She caught trains

and flew in planes.

She sailed on ships

and was chauffeured in cars.

Angela rode in buses, too.

She didn't want to miss a thing.

At a museum she admired an ancient pot.
"What beautiful creatures they had back then," said Angela.

While picnicking in the gardens of a royal palace,
something made her think of her own garden far away.

Angela was glad that she had brought her camera.

She wanted to photograph the interesting wildlife.

"I can't wait to show my photos to Old Tom," she said.

Angela visited an art gallery, where she saw a painting
that reminded her of home.

On a tour of the desert, Angela thought she saw Old Tom.
"It must be a mirage," she sighed, a little disappointed.

Angela had afternoon tea in an exclusive cafe.
But when Old Tom's favourite cakes arrived,
she wondered if tea for two might have been more fun.

By now, Angela was exhausted from all her travelling.
At a concert one night, she missed the
appearance of a surprise guest performer.

Then later, while strolling back to her hotel,
Angela was bewitched by a beautiful moon.

The following afternoon,
Angela noticed an unusual sunset.

She ought to have been having a wonderful time,
but something was missing.
"He's everywhere I look!" cried Angela Throgmorton,
as she ran to her room.

Angela was…lonely.

So she picked up the phone and rang Old Tom. But no one was home.
"He's out having fun," sobbed Angela. "Where could he be?"

At that very moment, a furry shape fell into her lap.
"Oh, my baby! What a wonderful surprise!"
Angela knew better than to ask any questions.

Instead, it was time to celebrate.

So she took Old Tom to a fancy restaurant.

"Order whatever you want!" said Angela Throgmorton.

And that is just what Old Tom did.

His table manners hadn't improved at all.

But for once Angela didn't mind…

…now that this was a holiday for two.

For David Francis and Julia Murray

Little Hare Books
4/21 Mary Street, Surry Hills
NSW 2010 AUSTRALIA

A CIP catalogue record for this book is available from the British Library.
ISBN 1 877003 02 6 (hardback)
ISBN 1 877003 22 0 (paperback)

Designed by ANTART
Printed in China

2 4 5 3 1